Clever Rachel

story by Debby Waldman

illustrations by Cindy Revell

ORCA BOOK PUBLISHERS

When Rachel, the innkeeper's daughter, was a baby, her father tucked her into bed not with lullabies but with riddles.

"That's crazy, *meshugganah*!" her mother said. "What does a baby know from riddles? I will sing to her."

But songs made Rachel wail. Fairy tales kept her awake. Riddles relaxed her, so riddles she heard.

To no one's surprise, Rachel's first sentence was a riddle. It was a simple riddle–"What crosses the river but cannot move?" And it made perfect sense. Just outside the inn was a wooden bridge that crossed the Olkinik River.

As Rachel grew up, her mother tried to teach her to sew, cook and keep house. But Rachel was more interested in riddles.

When her mother handed her a threaded needle and a scrap of muslin for her first embroidery project, Rachel asked, "What has an eye but never sees?" Then she refused to make even one stitch until her mother gave the correct answer: a needle.

When her mother tried to teach Rachel to make *kugel*, Rachel said, "I am a box with no corners or sides. I hold a golden treasure inside." Then she refused to roll out even one noodle until her mother gave the correct answer: an egg.

The first time Rachel's mother asked her to set out the candlesticks for the Shabbat table, Rachel said, "My life is short till I'm consumed. Wind will be my total ruin. I'm quickest when thin, slowest when fat, and I have scorched many a cat." Then she refused to set the table until her mother gave the correct answer: a candle.

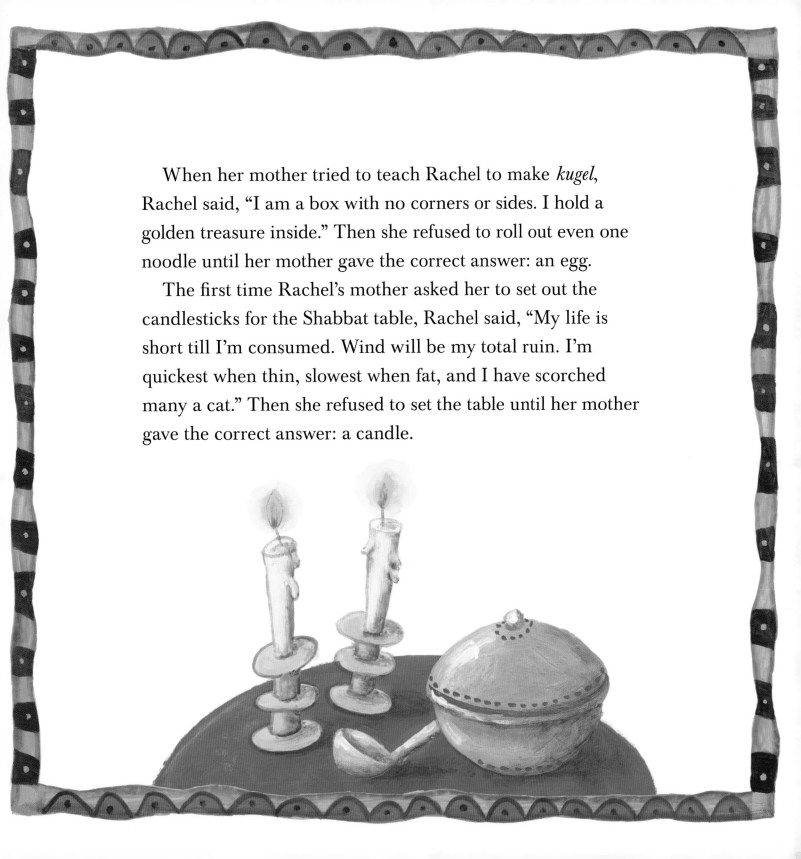

"Enough with the riddles!" her mother said. So Rachel found a new audience, visitors to the inn. They were charmed by her endless questions and answers. Some presented her with riddles that were as simple as the ones she'd made up as a little girl. Others brought riddles that were like mazes with more than one path to the end. But there were always people who were determined to stump her with tricky riddles. Into this category fell Jacob, son of Reb Wulff the baker.

Jacob went to school all week and studied the Talmud, which any scholar knows is full of some of the thorniest problems in the universe.

Rachel went to school too, but she studied sums and penmanship and candle blessings. Jacob knew this because his little sister, Hindy, went to the same school. Until Hindy started school, she had thought Jacob was the smartest person in the world. Not anymore. Now, all day long, it was *Clever Rachel this* and *Clever Rachel that*.

"Rachel can solve any riddle!" Hindy announced at dinner one night.

"Well, I was awarded the highest exam marks in school history!" Jacob reminded her.

"If Rachel had written those exams, she would have done even better than you!" Hindy said.

Impossible, Jacob thought. *No girl could be smarter than I am.* But just to be sure, he decided to visit Rachel.

The next afternoon, when he should have been studying, Jacob marched over to the inn. Rachel was doing sums in the dining room.

"What is the fastest thing?" Jacob asked her, not bothering to introduce himself. "What is the biggest thing? And what is harder to earn than money, but once you have it, can't be lost?"

Jacob barely had time to cross his arms over his chest before Rachel responded.

"The fastest thing is thought. The biggest thing is the earth. The hardest thing to earn is respect." She closed her book. "Have you more?" she asked politely. "I do love riddles."

Jacob was stunned. Rachel had devoured his best riddles
the way his father's customers devoured fresh *rugelach*.
He was about to say so when he was distracted by a loud noise
at the inn's door. Standing in the entry was a young woman,
who might have been beautiful had she not looked so distraught.

"My name is Miriam," she said. "I hear there is a clever child
at this inn. One who is good at solving riddles."

"I'm happy to help you," Rachel said, but Jacob's voice
was louder.

"My name is Jacob," he announced, stepping in front of
Rachel.

"But I'm the one you're looking for," Rachel protested.

Miriam didn't seem to hear her. She was too busy firing her
riddles at Jacob. "Impossible to touch but easy to feel, it's sweet
as honey and hard to conceal. What is it?"

Miriam didn't wait for an answer. "Small and round and made
of gold, it's a sign of promise since times of old. In a smithy's
shop it will linger, quietly waiting for just the right finger.
What is it?" Miriam asked. "And please, can you tell me,
what is a gift that is not a gift?"

Jacob couldn't find the answers as quickly as Miriam was asking the questions. So he stalled for time. "Why do you need help with these riddles?" he asked.

"Because I can't figure them out by myself," Miriam replied. She began to cry. Jacob, who was more comfortable with books and bread than with tearful maidens, turned away.

Rachel was as puzzled as Jacob. What was so important about these riddles? Why was it necessary to have the answers so quickly? But she didn't want to upset Miriam further with more questions. "Please sit while this clever boy solves your riddles," she said kindly, handing Miriam a cloth to dry her eyes. She glared at Jacob.

"Impossible to touch but easy to feel?" Jacob muttered. "Why couldn't she have easy riddles?"

"They're only hard because you don't know the answers," Rachel said, so quietly that no one could hear her.

"Do you know what a smithy makes that would linger?" Jacob whispered hopefully.

"I might," Rachel said.

"You don't!" he retorted.

"Neither do you," Rachel snapped.

"Please," Miriam interrupted. "I need my answers."

Rachel wanted so badly to solve the riddles. But that would mean helping the very boy who had come to the inn acting as if he was a king and she was his servant. If she helped Jacob, he'd take all the credit. She glared at him again. He'd gotten himself into this. He could get himself out.

The minutes ticked by. Miriam grew more agitated.

"I'm thinking," Jacob said. He put his hands over his ears and stared at the table, as if the answers lay in its knotted planks. "Impossible to touch but easy to feel…I know! It's the smell of lilacs on a spring afternoon!"

Miriam looked at him as if he were crazy. "How do you feel a smell? That can't be right."

It's love, Rachel thought to herself. But the words wouldn't leave her mouth.

"The thing that lingers in a smithy's shop—it's fire,"
Jacob continued as if Miriam hadn't spoken.

"Why would fire wait for a finger?" Miriam asked.
"Where is the wisdom in that?"

Jacob bit his lip. He wasn't used to being wrong.
He certainly wasn't used to having his answers criticized.
At school when his class was confronted with a thorny
problem, everyone talked about it until it made sense.
That's where true wisdom came from: working together.
"Two heads are better than one," the rabbi always said.
"And three, four and five are better still."

Jacob's face felt flushed and hot. "I am not the only clever child in this room," he admitted finally. "Rachel is the one you were looking for."

Miriam's face softened from anger to confusion. She turned to Rachel. "Then why have you been so quiet?"

Rachel wanted to say, *Because Jacob wouldn't let me speak,* but that wasn't quite true. Jacob had been rude and arrogant, but he hadn't taken away her voice. She had chosen not to speak, first because she was so surprised, and then because she was angry. She was still angry.

"I need help!" Miriam pleaded. "If I don't find the answers to these riddles, the man I love will be forced to marry another."

Rachel and Jacob did not understand.

"It is a tradition in his village," Miriam explained. "Before I can marry into his family, I must solve three riddles. Can't you put your differences aside long enough to help me?"

Rachel's anger melted into shame. To let pride get in the way of helping someone was worse than wrong. It was sinful. "The answer to the first riddle is love," she said. "You can't touch it, but you can feel it. And the sign of promise that lingers in a smithy's shop is a wedding ring."

She looked at Jacob to see if he agreed, but he was staring out the window at the birds pecking seeds in the yard.

"Doves!" Jacob said. "The gift that is not a gift. You present them in a cage, and when you open it to release them, they fly away."

"Thank you!" Miriam said, bowing deeply. And then she
was out the door.

Rachel and Jacob sat silently at the table. Clever though they were, they had little experience when it came to saying "I'm sorry."

It was Jacob who eventually spoke. "You really are wise," he said.

Rachel was about to respond when there was a loud noise at the inn's door. Standing in the entry was a frazzled-looking man.

"I must have the answers to three riddles by midnight," he said, his voice shaking. "I hear there is a clever child at this inn. One who is good at solving riddles."

This time it was Rachel who spoke loudly. "There are two clever children here," she said. "Come. Sit, and we will help you."

More Riddles for Rachel

Q: If I'm dropped, I'm sure to crack. But show me a smile, and I'll always smile back.

A: A mirror

Q: My hands have no fingers. My face has no eyes. I tick but can't talk to tell you time flies.

A: A clock

Q: I've caught many a kite, but my bark has no bite.

A: A tree

Q: If you're dirty and smelling sour, come stand near my trunk, and I'll give you a shower.

A: An elephant

Q: I fall from the cliffs but never break. I drop from the skies, and I fill up lakes.

A: Water

Q: I use a bank that has no money and a bed that has no sheets. I can run, but I have no feet. I have a mouth, but I cannot speak.

A: A river

Q: I have eighty-eight keys but don't need a lock. I have three pedals, and I'm shaped like a block.

A: A piano

A Note from Debby Waldman

I've always loved folktales. They link the past and present and offer readers and storytellers a different way to look at important ideas. *Clever Rachel* is my second Jewish folktale; *A Sack Full of Feathers* was the first. Both are set in Eastern Europe because my grandparents and great-grandparents grew up in "the old country." One of my favorite childhood memories is of watching my mother and my bubby— her mother—making rugelach, a traditional sweet treat. I put rugelach in my picturebooks because it's a way of keeping that memory alive forever.

Debby's Mother's Rugelach

1 cup butter, softened
2 cups sour cream (you can use low-fat, but not non-fat)
3–4 cups flour, as needed

Cream butter and sour cream. Mix in flour until the mixture pulls away from the sides of the bowl. After the dough is mixed, form it into discs. (This recipe will generate between 7 and 9 discs). Wrap each in plastic wrap or waxed paper, and refrigerate until firm—at least an hour. (You can also freeze it if you can't use it right away.)

1–2 cups cinnamon sugar (about two or more heaping teaspoons cinnamon per one cup sugar)
1–2 cups mini chocolate chips
1–2 cups walnuts
1–2 cups shredded coconut

Preheat oven to 350˚.

Coat your rolling surface with cinnamon sugar. Roll out the dough (on top of the cinnamon sugar) into a 14- to 16-inch circle. Slice the circle into wedges, pizza style. (Aim for between 12 and 16 wedges. Ideally each wedge will be 1.5 to 2 inches at the widest end). About half an inch in from the wide end, place about a teaspoon each of chips, walnuts and coconut. Roll up the wedges until you have a rugelach that resembles a small croissant. Roll the rugelach in cinnamon sugar, and place, end-side down, on a cookie sheet lined with parchment paper. Repeat until all the dough has been used.

Bake for 25 minutes, or until the rugelach are golden brown.

A tip: If the dough is difficult to roll out, sprinkle some flour onto the counter.
Another tip: The beauty of rugelach is that your filling choices are unlimited. My mother uses dates along with chocolate chips, walnuts and coconut. My friend Leah uses good-quality preserves. Whatever filling you choose, it must be thick enough that it won't get runny and leak.

For David, who is clever and wise. —D.W.

For Terry, who has a wickedly wonderful sense of humor. —C.R.

Library and Archives Canada Cataloguing in Publication

Waldman, Debby
Clever Rachel / story by Debby Waldman; illustrations by Cindy Revell.

ISBN 978-1-55469-323-8 (pbk.)
ISBN 978-1-55469-081-7 (bound)

I. Revell, Cindy, 1961- II. Title.
PS8645.A457C54 2009   JC813'.6   C2009-901660-5

First published in the United States, 2009
Library of Congress Control Number: 2009924734

Summary: In this retelling of a Jewish folktale, Rachel and Jacob must work together to solve the trickiest riddles of all.

Orca Book Publishers gratefully acknowledges the support for its publishing programs provided by the following agencies: the Government of Canada through the Canada Book Fund and the Canada Council for the Arts, and the Province of British Columbia through the BC Arts Council and the Book Publishing Tax Credit.

Cover artwork by Cindy Revell
Design by Teresa Bubela

ORCA BOOK PUBLISHERS
orcabook.com

Printed and bound in South Korea.

23 22 21 20 • 7 6 5 4

072033.1K1/B290/A7